WHEN I AM EIGHT

· JOAN LOWERY NIXON ·

Pictures by DICK GACKENBACH

DIAL BOOKS FOR YOUNG READERS

NEW YORK

Published by Dial Books for Young Readers
A Division of Penguin Books USA Inc.
375 Hudson Street
New York, New York 10014

Designed by Julie Rauer
Printed in Hong Kong
First Edition
1 3 5 7 9 10 8 6 4 2

Library of Congress Cataloging in Publication Data
Nixon, Joan Lowery.
When I am eight / by Joan Lowery Nixon;
pictures by Dick Gackenbach.—1st ed.
p.   cm.
Summary: A child imagines how things will be
when he is eight, like his big brother.
ISBN 0-8037-1499-8 (tr.)—ISBN 0-8037-1500-5 (lib. bdg.)
[1. Growth—Fiction.   2. Brothers—Fiction.   3. Imagination—
Fiction.]   I. Gackenbach, Dick, ill.   II. Title.
PZ7.N65Wg   1994   [E]—dc20   93-20023   CIP   AC

The art was rendered in a pen-and-ink line
with Dr. Martin's concentrated watercolors.

To Bridget Elizabeth Quinlan,
with my love
J. L. N.

When *I* am eight, like my brother, I'll get a big bike too. Just like his.

BUT…

My bike will have super-zowie hotshot light-up power pedals that won't fit his big feet. Only mine. Then when my brother says, "You're too little to ride my bike," I'll say, "Who cares?"

My bike will have ten flags, not just one, and balloons and streamers and a sign that says HERE GOES THE BEST BIKE RIDER IN THE WHOLE WORLD.

I'll do figure eights and wheelies and ride so fast that people will have to hold on to things to keep from falling over. They'll yell, "Who was *that*?"

And my brother will say, "Wow!"

When *I* am eight.

When *I* am eight, like my brother, I'll get a new baseball and bat and glove too. Just like his.

BUT…

My ball and bat and glove will come in a box with a sign on top that says EVERYTHING IN THIS BOX IS FOR THE BEST BASEBALL PLAYER IN THE WHOLE WORLD AND NOT FOR HIS BIG BROTHER. Then when my brother says, "You can't play ball with us because you're too little," I'll say, "Who cares?"

My ball will be autographed by every baseball player in the major leagues. And my bat will have my name printed on it in letters so big that people will see it a block away. Two blocks. Maybe even three.

I'll knock the dirt off my shoes with the end of my bat, like the ball players do on TV. Then I'll swing my bat over my shoulder. And when the pitch comes, I'll hit the ball so hard that it will go higher than the house. Higher than ten houses.

People going by in an airplane will see it. And
everybody will cheer and shout, "Yeaaaa, Herbie!"
And my brother will say, "Wow!"
When *I* am eight.

When *I* am eight, like my brother, I'll get a video game too. Just like his.

BUT...

My video game will be so hard to play that he can't do it. Only me. Then when my brother says, "You're too little to know how to play my video game," I'll say, "Who cares?"

In *my* video game real monsters
with giant claws will leap out at
each side, and big spiders will drop
from the top, and crabs with
pincher claws will crawl up from the
bottom. But I'll zap them into a
million pieces.

There'll be music, and lights will
flash, and next to my name will be
THIS IS THE BEST SCORE IN THE
WHOLE WORLD.

All the kids in the neighborhood
will say, "I wish I could do that!"

And my brother will say, "Wow!"

When *I* am eight.

When *I* am eight, like my brother, I'll go to school with a box of birthday cupcakes too. Just like his.

BUT…

I'll bring so many cupcakes that everybody in *my* class can eat as many as they want and take a lot home to give to their brothers and sisters. Then when my brother says, "You're too little to come to my school and you can't have a cupcake because there aren't enough," I'll say, "Who cares?"

My cupcakes will be bigger than anybody has ever seen. They'll have frosting outside *and* inside. Chocolate and vanilla. And on top they'll have colored sprinkles and gumdrops and chocolate-covered peanuts and jelly beans. And on the box it will say THESE ARE THE BEST BIRTHDAY CUPCAKES IN THE WHOLE WORLD.

Everybody in my class will yell and clap their hands.

And my brother will say, "Wow!"

When *I* am eight.

When *I* am eight, like my brother, I'll have a birthday party too. Just like his.

BUT…

At my birthday party I'll invite everybody in the neighborhood. Maybe everybody in the school. But they can't come if they don't bring their little brothers and sisters. Then when my brother says, "Mom, he's too little to sit with us," I'll say, "Who cares?"

At *my* birthday party I'll have a circus in the backyard and ponies to ride in the front yard. There'll be clowns and magicians and balloons. And a parade.

An elephant will carry a sign that says
THIS IS THE BEST BIRTHDAY PARTY IN THE
WHOLE WORLD.

The birthday cake will be so big that I'll have to stand on a ladder to blow out the candles.

And everybody will cheer and sing "Happy Birthday" to me.

And my brother will say, "Wow!"

When *I* am eight.

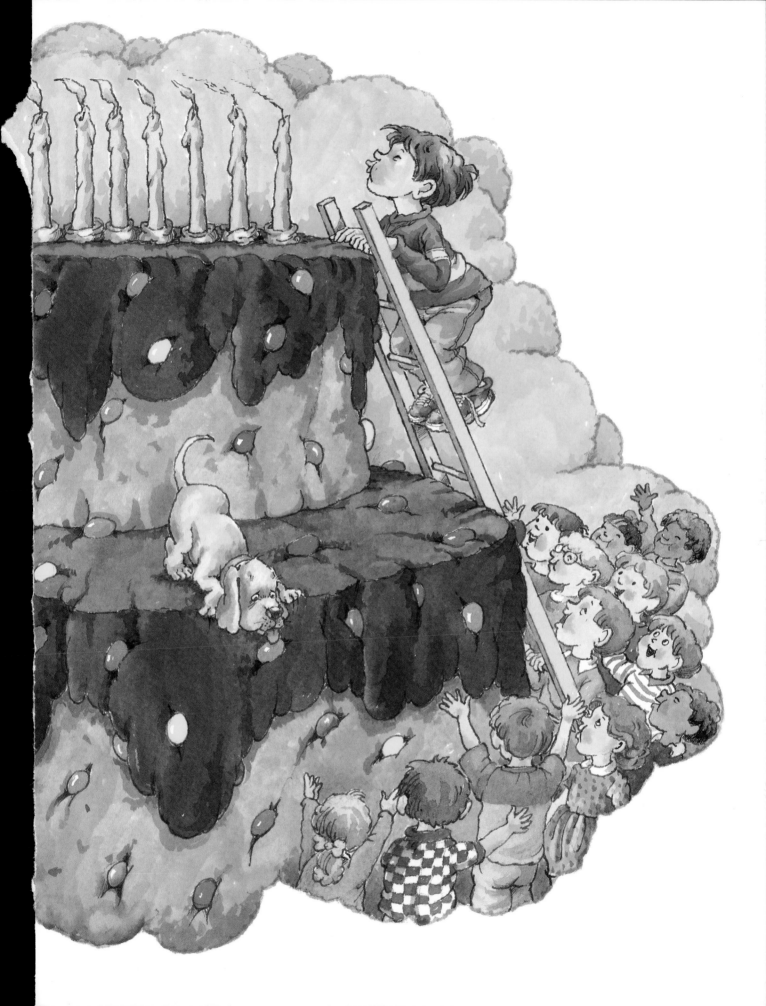

When *I* am eight, I'll give my brother some birthday cake and ice cream too, but *I* won't make *him* eat it in the kitchen with Mom.

He can come to my party even if he *is* bigger and stronger and older than me. Even if he keeps telling me I'm too little. Even if he keeps making me SO MAD! Because he *is* my brother.

BUT...
It will be *my* birthday and not his.
When *I* am eight!

E   Nixon, Joan Lowery ✓
NIX   When I am eight

                              39545000461078

$13.99